Moke and Poki
in the Rain Forest
by Mamoru Funai

An I CAN READ Book

Harper & Row, Publishers
New York, Evanston, San Francisco, London

For Ellen Rudin

MOKE AND POKI IN THE RAIN FOREST
Copyright © 1972 by Mamoru Funai

Trade Standard Book Number: 06-021926-2
Harpercrest Standard Book Number: 06-021927-0
Library of Congress Catalog Card Number: 72-76510
FIRST EDITION

Contents

Moke and Poki Build a House   5
Moke Sings to the Moon   20
The Bean-Pod Canoe   34
The Rainbow   50

The people and animals in this book
live in the State of Hawaii. Some of
the words in this book are Hawaiian
words. Here is how to say them.

 Moke (MOH-keh) a name

Poki (POH-kee) another name

 Menehunes (Meh-neh-HOO-neez) little people

Menehune (Meh-neh-HOO-nee)
one little person

 Taro (TA-roh) a plant that grows in Hawaii

Aloha (Ah-LOH-hah) greetings; love; welcome; farewell

 Nene-goose (NAY-nay goos)
the state bird of Hawaii

Moke and Poki Build a House

The menehunes

lived in the rain forest.

Moke was a menehune.

He was six inches tall.

He lived in a bush.

One day

Moke told his friend Poki,

"I am tired of

living in a bush."

"You are silly," said Poki.

"But I want to live

in a real house,"

said Moke.

6

"Where can you find a real house

in the rain forest?"

asked Poki.

"Come, we will look for a house,"

said Moke.

Moke and Poki looked everywhere,

but they could not find a house.

"We did not see one house,"

said Poki.

"Then I will build a house,"

said Moke.

"I will help you,

but only because

you are my friend," said Poki.

So Moke and Poki

started to build the house.

Along came Crayfish.

"I will help you build the house,"
said Crayfish.

In a little while, Nene-goose flew by.

"I will help you build the house,"
said Nene-goose.

Dog saw them building the house.

"I can help too," said Dog.

Cricket came and decided to help.

In a few hours

the house was finished.

"Thank you for all your help,"

said Moke. "Now I have

a real house, and it is all mine."

"No, it is not all yours,"

said Crayfish. "I helped,

so it is my house too."

"It is mine too," said Nene-goose.

"I helped!" said Dog.

"So did I," said Cricket.

"Well then," said Moke,

"we will all live in the house."

"Not everyone," said Poki. "I want

to stay in my house in the bush."

That night,

Moke, Crayfish, Nene-goose,

Dog, and Cricket

went to live in the new house.

It began to rain.

Nene-goose felt a raindrop

on his head.

14

"I am getting wet," said Nene-goose.

Nene-goose changed places with Dog.

"Now I am getting wet," said Dog.

Dog changed places with Cricket.

"My wings are getting wet,"

said Cricket.

"I don't mind getting wet,"

said Crayfish.

He changed places with Cricket.

It began to rain even harder.

Water came in from everywhere.

Soon the roof caved in,

and the walls fell apart.

Everyone ran for the nearest bush.

It was Poki's house.

"Help us up," said Moke.

"Do you have any room up there?"

asked Dog.

"There is plenty of room,"

said Poki.

And so everyone

climbed up the bush.

They found a place in the branches.

They pulled the leaves

over their heads

and went to sleep together.

Moke Sings to the Moon

Moke sang to the moon.

He sang as loud as he could.

"What are you doing?"

asked Nene-goose.

"Can't you tell?" said Moke. "I am

singing to the moon."

"Oh," said Nene-goose.

"Can I sing too?"

"Of course you can, Nene-goose."

20

And so Moke and Nene-goose

sang to the moon.

"Wait a minute," said Moke.

"Something is wrong.

Somebody is singing out of tune."

Just then Cricket came by.

"What are you doing?" he asked.

"Can't you tell?"

said Nene-goose. "We are

singing to the moon."

"Can I sing too?" said Cricket.

"Of course," said Moke.

And so Moke, Nene-goose,

and Cricket sang to the moon.

"Wait a minute. Something is wrong.

Somebody is singing

out of tune," said Moke.

Along came Dog and Green Frog.

"Oh, look! They are singing

to the moon," said Dog.

"Why are you singing to the moon?"

asked Green Frog.

"Because the moon is the only one

who would listen," said Moke.

"Of course," said Green Frog.

"How silly of me to ask."

"We want to sing too,"

said Dog and Green Frog.

"All right," said Moke.

So everyone sang to the moon.

"Wait a minute," said Moke.

"Something is wrong.

Somebody is singing out of tune."

"Let us sing one at a time,"

said Dog. "That way we can hear

who is singing out of tune."

Nene-goose sang.

"No, it is not Nene-goose,"

said Moke.

Cricket sang.

"No, it is not Cricket," said Moke.

Dog and Green Frog sang.

"No, it is not Dog or Green Frog,"

said Moke.

Then Moke sang.

"It is Moke!

Moke is singing out of tune,"

said Dog.

Moke felt bad.

"I will not sing with you anymore.

I do not want to ruin another song,"

he said.

He was very sad.

"I know!" said Dog.

"You can be our conductor."

"Every chorus needs a conductor,"

said Nene-goose.

"Yes, that is a good idea,"

said Cricket.

And so, Moke became the conductor,

and he led the chorus in a song.

Later when everyone had gone,

Moke sat and looked at the moon.

The moon shone brightly down on him.

He then sang as loud as he could.

The Bean-Pod Canoe

Moke and Poki walked through
the vegetable garden.
"Look at those plants,"
said Moke. "They are so big!"
"And just look at those cucumbers,"
said Poki.
"These tomatoes are
as big as a house," said Moke.

"Look at the beans. They are
as big as a canoe," said Poki.

"A canoe?" said Moke.

"You know. A canoe that can sail
in the water," said Poki.

"I know what a canoe is," said Moke.

"I have an idea.

Let us take a bean

and make a canoe out of it."

"Good idea!" said Poki. "And

we can sail it out on the sea."

"Yes, but we better hurry,"

said Moke. "It is getting dark."

Moke and Poki climbed the vines

and cut down the largest bean.

They opened and cleaned the bean.

Moke and Poki

carried the bean-pod canoe

over their heads.

"There is the sea," said Moke.

"We are lucky," said Poki.

"It floats."

Moke and Poki found two flat leaves

from a bush.

"This can be a paddle," said Moke.

Moke and Poki climbed into
the bean-pod canoe.
They paddled the canoe
far out into the water.

They sang this song:

> We are sailing, sailing,
>
> Sailing out to sea.
>
> There is no place on earth
>
> We would rather be
>
> Than sailing, sailing,
>
> Sailing out to sea.

Dark clouds began to cover

the twinkling stars.

There was thunder and lightning.

The bean-pod canoe

tossed up and down.

"Hurry! Bail out the water,"

shouted Moke.

Moke and Poki splashed the water out

as fast as they could.

Up and down went the bean-pod canoe.

"I think I am getting sick,"

said Poki.

"Don't get sick now," said Moke.

"Just bail out the water."

44

"Can you swim?" asked Poki.

"No, not yet," said Moke.

"Well, neither can I," said Poki.

"Faster! Faster! Keep bailing!"

shouted Moke.

More water came in.

The bean-pod canoe

began to sink

into the water.

"It is no use," said Moke.

"This is the end," said Poki.

"This is good-bye," said Moke.

"Aloha," said Poki.

"Aloha, my friend," said Moke.

The bean-pod canoe

sank lower and lower.

Then suddenly it stopped sinking.

"What happened?" said Poki.

"We have reached the bottom,"

said Moke.

"This is not a very deep ocean,"
said Poki.

"Yes, but I am glad it is not,"
said Moke. "Come, Poki,
let's go home."

Moke and Poki stepped out

of the bean-pod canoe

and walked back to shore.

The rain was over.

The stars were twinkling

in the sky again.

The Rainbow

Moke sat on a rock.

He stared into the rain valley.

He sat there for a long time.

Then he sang this song:

Rainbow, rainbow in the skies.

Pretty colors in my eyes.

There is red and there is blue,

Yellow, green, and purple too.

50

"What are you doing?" said Poki.

"I am waiting for the rainbow,"
said Moke.

"A rainbow!" said Poki. "What a
silly thing to do."

Nene-goose, Mouse,

Dog, and Green Frog

came from the forest.

"What are you doing?" said Mouse.

"I am waiting for the rainbow,"

said Moke.

"That is the silliest thing

I ever heard," said Nene-goose.

"There must be better things to do."

Dog and Green Frog began to laugh.

"A rainbow! Ha, ha, ha, ha!

That's funny."

"Come on," said Poki,

"let us go and play."

Poki, Nene-goose, Mouse,

Dog, and Green Frog

walked into the rain forest.

Soon it began to rain,

and everyone ran under a plant.

"Well, what shall we do?"

said Nene-goose.

"Oh, there must be

many things we can do," said Poki.

"Can you think of something to do?"

asked Mouse.

"No, not right now," said Dog.

"Well, neither can I," said Green Frog.

They watched the rain

falling on the ground.

They watched the raindrops

dripping from the leaves.

"I wonder why Moke wanted to see
a rainbow," said Nene-goose.
"Maybe it is because
he has never seen a rainbow,"
said Poki.
"Have you seen a rainbow?"
asked Mouse.
"I am not sure," said Nene-goose.

"Come to think of it," said Poki,

"I have never seen a rainbow."

"Me neither," said Dog.

"Neither have I," said Green Frog.

"Well, what are we waiting for,"

said Poki.

Moke was sitting on the rock

with a wide leaf over his head.

"Did the rainbow come?" said Poki.

"Not yet," said Moke.

"May we stay?" said Poki.

"Please do," said Moke.

Poki, Nene-goose, Mouse,

Dog, and Green Frog

sat under Moke's wide leaf.

They stared into the rain valley.

Soon the sun

peeked through the clouds.

A beautiful rainbow came.

Then another and another.

The rain valley

was filled with rainbows.

Moke and his friends were so happy.

They clapped their hands.

Then they sang this song:

> Rainbows, rainbows in the skies.
>
> Pretty colors in our eyes.
>
> When it rains and we can't play,
>
> We watch rainbows all the day.

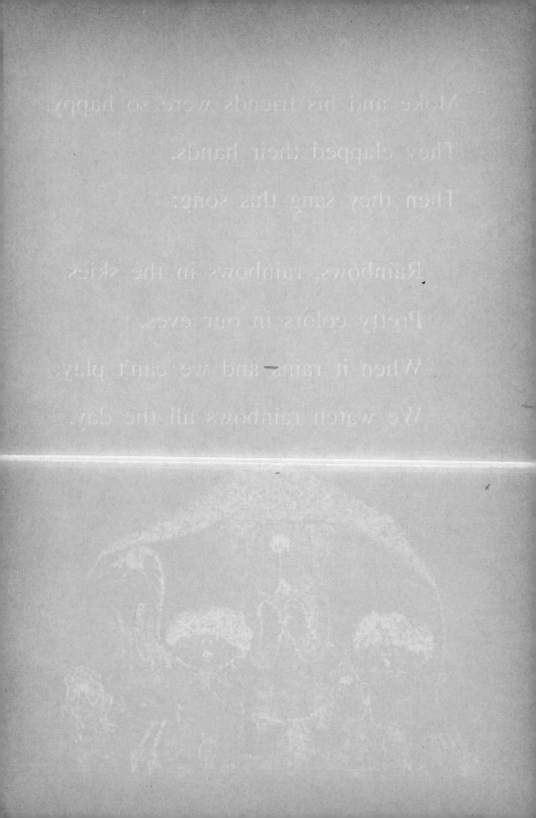